AN OMNIBUS

BOSS OF

Shelley thinks she's old enough [...]
own while her mother works at a hostel for
mentally and physically handicapped children.
Shelley's mum, Anne, doesn't agree. In the
ensuing battle Shelley learns some painful lessons
about herself and gains a greater understanding
of others. This story of a girl's attempts to
teach a retarded boy to swim will touch anyone
who reads it.

Robin Klein
Boss of the Pool

AN OMNIBUS/PUFFIN BOOK

The author wishes to thank the Literature Board of the Australia Council for the grant which enabled her to work on this and other manuscripts

Text artwork by Helen Panagopoulos

Omnibus Books
255 Pulteney Street
Adelaide, South Australia, 5000
Australia

Penguin Books Australia Ltd,
487 Maroondah Highway, P.O. Box 257
Ringwood, Victoria, 3134, Australia
Penguin Books Ltd,
Harmondsworth, Middlesex, England
Penguin Books,
40 West 23rd Street, New York, N.Y. 10010 U.S.A.
Penguin Books Canada Ltd,
2801 John Street, Markham, Ontario, Canada
Penguin Books (N.Z.) Ltd,
182–190 Wairau Road, Auckland 10, New Zealand

First published by Omnibus Books, 1986
Published by Penguin Books, Australia, in association with Omnibus Books, 1986
Reprinted 1987 (twice)
Reprinted 1988
Text copyright © Robin Klein
Illustrations copyright © Omnibus Books

Typeset in Australia by Caxtons, Adelaide
Made and printed in Australia by
The Book Printer, Maryborough, Victoria

CIP

Klein, Robin
  Boss of the pool
  ISBN 0 14 032246 9
  I. Title.
A823'.3

CONTENTS

DEDICATION

for Clemence and Morgan

CHAPTER ONE

At first Anne tried coaxing. "You'd really like it, Shelley," she said. "They have table tennis and a craft room and a lovely indoor pool."

But Shelley translated the coaxing into brainwashing. "I'm not coming," she said angrily. "I already told you a million times that I want to stay home by myself! I don't see why I'm not allowed. Petra Van Rees stays home by herself two whole nights a week when her mum goes to aerobics."

"I don't care what Petra does." Her mother's voice shed some of its patience. "You're not old enough to be left alone in the evenings, even if it is only till 9.45. That house round the corner got broken into last month . . ."

"As if anyone would want to bust into our house! As if there's anything here worth pinching!" Shelley regretted saying that, for her mother's face looked suddenly hurt and vulnerable, but the regret didn't last for more than a few seconds. She was too angry. "Having to go next door to stay with that boring old Mrs Murray every single night for the rest of the holidays!"

"You know I'll be having Sunday evenings off."

"Big deal! Megan Webb is going away to the Gold Coast. We never go anywhere posh like that! I don't know why you can't get a proper job, anyhow. Petra's mum has a great one managing a music shop and Petra gets cassettes half-price any time she wants, and she's going away for the holidays, too. Anyway, even if she wasn't, I bet she wouldn't have to go next door and stay with a boring old lady when she could be home in her own place watching television!"

"I've already said that you can come with me to the nursing home and use the pool there. You don't *have* to go to Mrs Murray's every night. And Shelley, you should realise that I was lucky to get this job. Any job. I'm not really qualified for anything in particular. Anyhow, I can't stay here arguing; I've got to leave in five minutes. If you're sure you won't change your mind and come with me, then run along over to Mrs Murray's. And for goodness sake, stop that silly sulking."

Shelley stormed next door with a face as fierce as a hawk and rang Mrs Murray's doorbell, determined to find no pleasure in the three hours' enforced stay. Mrs Murray was a cheerful, kind, aunty sort of person. As soon as Shelley was sitting down she got out the album of her son's recent wedding. Shelley glanced through it, making hardly any effort to disguise her boredom. When Mrs Murray made tea and produced a plate of delectable sponge fingers, Shelley took only one and said that she wasn't hungry. She kept her nose in a library book, even though it was dull, and resisted Mrs Murray's attempts at conversation.

9

"Some kind of nursing home, is it, where your mum's working now?" Mrs Murray asked, comfortably knitting away at a baby's jacket for her daughter's expected baby. "I think your mum's wonderful to take on a job like that."

"It's a sort of hostel. I don't know much about it. You'll have to ask her when she gets home," Shelley said curtly, pretending that she'd reached an exciting part of the book and didn't want to be interrupted. She felt ashamed that Anne was working in such a place. None of the other kids at school had mothers working in a job like that.

"A hostel for mentally and physically handicapped people," Mrs Murray said, maddeningly chatty.

Shelley didn't answer and flipped over an unread page. She should be able to see that I'm too annoyed

10

to chat, too annoyed to do anything except huddle in the middle of my rage, she thought.

"She'll be tired when she gets home. I should imagine handicapped people are very exhausting to work with. She's lucky she's got you, Shelley, to help her with the housework and that." Mrs Murray switched on the television for the 8.30 film.

Shelley watched impatiently for ten minutes and decided that the film was the sloppiest she'd ever seen.

"Can I use your phone, please?" she asked, heading towards the hallway and the phone table before Mrs Murray had even nodded.

She phoned Petra, who was starry with excitement because she was going away for a holiday at a children's country guest house. Shelley tried to sound interested, but felt overwhelmed by jealously and self-pity. It wasn't fair! Her mother hadn't been able to afford a holiday, and now she would be on duty at that wretched hostel for four weeks, too. Four weeks of spending every evening with Mrs Murray! It just wasn't fair!

She cut Petra short in the middle of eagerly reading aloud the holiday brochure. "I've got to go now," Shelley lied. "I promised I'd give Denise a ring tonight."

But it was just as bad talking to Denise, whose cousins were staying for the holidays. She chattered on about outings to the beach, a tour of some lighthouse, a dozen other glittering things. "What are you doing over the holidays, Shelley?" she asked finally, running out of breath.

Shelley scowled into the phone and launched into a

long tirade. "Mum has this stupid job," she said resentfully. "She's something called an occupational therapy aide at some nursing home place. So every night I've got to stay with Mrs Murray next door. Mum won't even let me stay in our house by myself!" It was a hint for Denise to invite her over to stay tomorrow, but Denise, filled with the glamour of having visiting interstate cousins and a hectic social whirl, didn't notice the hint.

"Poor you," she said with easy sympathy. "It must

be boring. But look on the bright side—when school starts again you'll know how to crochet!"

"Very funny," Shelley said coldly.

"I've got to hang up now, Shel. Uncle Bruce is taking us all down to the Pizza Hut for tea. See ya."

After ringing Megan and getting no answer, Shelley glared at the living room door, sighed, and went back inside. Mrs Murray was waiting with a huge box of photos of her three grown-up children taken at the time they had all been at school.

Every night at 6.00 when Anne left for work, she reissued the invitation for Shelley to go along with her to the hostel. "You keep saying how bored you are at Mrs Murray's," she pointed out. "Come on, darling, give it a try. There's a whole pool over there going to waste. It's better than sitting next door scowling at poor old Mrs Murray when she's only being kind enough to help me out."

"Why can't she come in here for a change?" Shelley demanded furiously. "She could watch our TV and I could stay in my room and not have to talk to her."

"Oh, Shelley, do stop going on about it! Of course I can't expect her to trail in here every night and be deafened by those awful loud cassettes of yours! Please be reasonable about it. She's the one doing us a favour, and I'm certainly not going to ask her to get out of her routine while she's doing it."

"Her routine! All she ever does is look at stupid old photos and watch daggy films on the telly," Shelley scoffed. "That's bad enough, but going to that creepy nursing home would be even worse! I won't do it!"

13

But next afternoon Mrs Murray called apologetically to say that she would have to go to Albury. Her daughter had had the new baby.

"More baby photos for me to look at when she gets back!" Shelley thought bitterly, and then brightened as she realised that now she would be able to stay home all by herself. There was no alternative. "I'll ask Denise and Megan around," she thought. "And Petra, if she hasn't gone to the holiday ranch yet. We'll have the sound up really loud and no one will be around to tell us to turn it down!"

But Anne had other ideas. "I won't let you stay in the house alone after dark," she said. "And it wouldn't make any difference if you had all your school friends here. You'll have to come along with me to the hostel, and there's no point arguing about it."

Shelley sulked all afternoon and was still sulking when they drove to the hostel. It was a long cream brick building which took up the whole side of a little side street, stretching from corner to corner.

"No wonder!" Shelley jeered. "Who'd want to build their house right next door to those freaky people in the nursing home?"

Anne didn't say anything. She collected her handbag and a big box of coloured raffia from the back seat and opened the car door. Shelley sat with her arms folded, staring straight ahead. "I'm not coming in," she said defiantly. "I'll wait for you out here. There's no way anyone's going to make me go in *there*!"

"Suit yourself, then," Anne said. "Just don't you

dare tell me you've been bored when I come off duty, that's all!"

Boredom came swiftly. Shelley had brought along two tapes and played them one after the other until she grew heartily tired of both. She filed her nails and tried out a new hairstyle in the glovebox mirror. Suddenly she became aware that someone was looking at her. Not looking, staring. Her hands, busily doing things to her hair, grew uneasily still.

She looked back. Stared back, feeling that staring was a justified reaction to such a strange face.

The boy was pressed like a dead autumn leaf against the glass front door of the hostel. The palms of his hands were flattened out, and his eyes, framed by the square they made, stared at Shelley intently and without blinking.

She wished that her mother hadn't parked the car on the nature strip so close to the front entrance. She quickly shifted over to the driving seat, so that she was slightly out of his range of vision and didn't have to look at him or even acknowledge that he was there. It was the polite thing to do, surely, to pretend that someone wasn't there, when they had a face like that, she thought.

When her mother came off duty at 9.30, Shelley moved angrily over to her own side. "About time, too! How *can* you work in a place like that, when it's full of spooks!"

16

Shelley spent most of the following day ringing up all the girls in her class and angling for invitations to stay the night. Liz was going to a film with her family; Petra had already left for her holiday; Denise was sharing her room with one of her cousins; there was no answer at all from Megan's house. At 6 o'clock Shelley still hadn't found a refuge, and would have actually welcomed Mrs Murray's return from Albury.

"Hurry up, Shelley, or I'll be late for work," her mother called. Shelley trailed dismally out to the car and banged the door after her, maintaining a stony silence all the way to the hostel. Anne parked the car, hesitated, and said gently, "Shelley, won't you come in and say hello to the kids?"

Shelley didn't bother to answer. She opened her library book and began to read and her mother went into the hostel alone.

The library book was no more interesting than the one she'd read at Mrs Murray's, and something had gone wrong with the cassette player, making the tapes crackle with static. There was nothing else to do except read the street directory. She kept her head down. That weird-looking boy was plastered against the door again, staring out at her. They shouldn't let people like that stand about where ordinary, normal people had to look at them! It wasn't right!

She grew conscious of a need to visit a bathroom, and tried to ignore it. Eventually she had to leave the car and go to the front door of the hostel. She peered warily past the large boy with his disturbing face, hoping to see her mother, but the foyer was empty. There was nothing else to do except knock. The boy beamed at her horribly and fiddled about with a complicated deadlock to open the door.

He's weird, Shelley thought, utterly gross, and the worst thing is that he doesn't even seem to realise it himself! He grinned happily, as though she had finally decided to come out of the car just to pay him a visit.

"Where's the toilet?" she muttered. He grabbed her arm and pulled her helpfully down a long corridor. Shelley looked about frantically for her mother, but the corridor was deserted. At its end, thank goodness, was a Ladies sign on a bathroom door.

"Thanks for showing me," Shelley said, putting all the dismissal she could into the words. She shut the door in his face and spent a long time in the bathroom, giving him plenty of time to go away. She washed her hands and combed her hair in front of the mirror, She tried her vee-neck shirt on back to front to see if it would look smart, the way Megan had been wearing all her vee-neck shirts this summer. It only looked stupid, so she put it on the right way around. At least she'd given that terrible kid ample time to take himself

off to wherever people who looked like that went in their spare time, she thought.

She tiptoed to the door and opened it carefully, ready to make a dash along the corridor and out through the front door and the safety of the car.

"You took long time," he said, standing with formidable patience just outside the door. "Whazz your name?"

"Shelley, though it's none of your business," she said, stepping around him.

"Berry?"

"*Shelley!*"

She hurried up the corridor and tugged at the front door. It didn't budge, and the locking mechanism was complicated. She looked back. The boy was still standing by the bathroom door, gazing after her wistfully. Shelley tugged urgently at the door again.

"Are you Anne Treloar's daughter?" asked someone in a white uniform, emerging from one of the rooms along the corridor. "You don't have to wait out in the car, dear. It must be so boring out there for you. Would you like a cup of tea? Supper's on now, in the big room. Ben, take Shelley through, will you, love?"

Shelley tried to think of an excuse, anything at all, not to have to go through those inner glass doors, into that room full of people she could just see from the corners of her horrified eyes. No way would she go into that room! There was someone, something, in a wheelchair, with both cheeks disfigured by a huge dark birthmark, and there was her mother, calmly helping that person, that thing, to cordial and biscuits! The room seemed, to her panic-stricken eyes, to be full of grotesque people, moving as though in slow motion, gesturing in strange uncoordinated ways. Some of them were quite small children, but not like any children she'd ever seen. And the adults among them were like badly distorted photographs of proper adults, taken with a faulty camera. She peered, appalled, at a hideously stunted woman who scuttled aimlessly like a spider along the wall from chair to chair, vacant eyes, nightmare hands clutching . . . She couldn't possibly go into that dreadful room!

A hand reached out and took hers. "Smerry *my* friend," the boy said. "She come see *me*. She come see my room, my posters and bear and that."

"No, I don't really want to, thanks very much!" Shelley protested, but she was hauled back along the corridor. His room was right at the end, with a number on its door. While she was thinking how awful it must

21

be to have a number on your bedroom, as though you were a letter in a post office mailbox, he flung open its door with a tremendous, baffling pride.

She glanced briefly at the posters of some dated pop group on the walls, and a teddy bear in a football scarf and pom-pom hat on the bed. There was a large coloured print of Prince Charles and Princess Diana. The rest of the room was just cupboards, linoleum, and a certain chilly tidiness. The boy, who was too big to be a child, picked the bear up and held it under her nose.

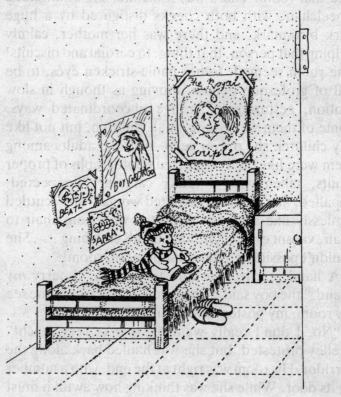

"Richmond," he said. "Tigers. What your team? What you say your name?"

"Shelley. I already told you twice," Shelley said irritably, not looking at the bear. "And I don't barrack for any football team. I hate football, and I've got to go now, anyhow. Goodbye."

She looked out, to make sure that the nurse with her relentless hospitality was no longer in the foyer, then sped along the corridor to the door. Thankfully the lock clicked back, the door opened and she slipped through. But not before Ben planted a large wet kiss on her ear.

Shelley dived into the car and slammed the door. She scrabbled through the glovebox for a tissue and scrubbed away at her ear, thinking that at any moment she might be sick. He was still there, watching, doing his depressing autumn leaf imitation against the glass. But this time one hand was moving, waving to her, waving, waving. It looked just like someone drowning she thought, someone drowning and summoning a life guard at the beach.

She picked up the street directory and hid behind it so she wouldn't have to wave back.

CHAPTER THREE

"You know very well you never use those old building blocks or the dolls' house," Anne said. "They were just cluttering up the garage. I wish you'd stop this . . ."

"Stop what?" Shelley demanded, meshed in bad-tempered thoughts of the pointless riding about on her bike she'd done that day. Rebecca had been in bed with a sore throat and high temperature; no one was home at Megan's place; Liz had Paula over to stay and they quite clearly hadn't wanted Shelley barging in on their gossip and secrets. "Stop what? I think you've got a nerve giving *them* my old toys!"

"They've hardly got any equipment there. I would have thought that an old set of building blocks . . ."

"Playing with blocks at their age!" Shelley jeered. "There's one kid there looks about fifteen or sixteen and he talks like a baby. Don't expect me to help carry in my blocks and the dolls' house when I never even gave you permission to give them away, anyhow. Not to people like that!"

"So we're going to sit for three hours sulking again, are we?" Anne said distantly as she parked the car.

"No, I'm not! I'm going to use that dumb pool, if you want to know," Shelley said. "I'm not going to be bored out of my mind again, coming to this spooky place every evening when I don't even want to. I'm going to stay in the pool till you finish, but only if there's just me in it. If any of those people come, I'll get straight out and come back to the car. Oh God, look who's waiting at the door!"

When Ben saw the car, his face creased up into an immense grin, and Shelley could see his mouth forming into a shout to match it. "*Mary*!" That's what he was yelling soundlessly from behind the glass.

"Especially if *he* goes in the pool," she snapped. "If he goes swimming, I won't stay in there a second."

"Ben never goes anywhere near the pool," Anne said. "He's petrified of water, poor darling. All the nurses have tried to get him to go in, but he won't even put a foot in to paddle. That's how scared he is. I don't think any of the others will be using the pool, either, as there's usually no one free to supervise after 6.30. Just pick up the key to the pool door from the nurse's desk along that passage. See you later, Shelley."

"Cherry, where you been long time, you bad girl!" Ben said.

Strewth! thought Shelley. Maybe he thinks I'm one of those gross kids who *lives* here!

"Hello, Ben," Anne said, smiling at him. "Did you have a nice day?"

Nice? thought Shelley. What a tactless thing to say! As if anyone looking like him could possibly have a nice day! She edged cautiously around Ben with her beachbag and towel. When he saw what she was

26

carrying, his face filled with alarm.

"Not go!" he said urgently. "No! She drown! Mary *drown*!"

Anne caught him gently and put an arm around him. "No one could drown in that pool, darling," she said. "It's not deep enough. Anyhow, Shelley can swim really well. She's got a big gold medal she won in swimming. So how about coming along with me to finish painting the mural with Tania and Greg?"

Shelley fled from Ben's voice babbling "Mary drown! Mary drown!" over and over. She found the nurse's desk, explained who she was and asked for the pool door key. The nurse smiled at her, but Shelley didn't smile back. She was too intent on escaping through that heavy metal door and locking it firmly behind her—locking out Ben's voice. He was still wailing at the other end of the corridor, with her mum trying to comfort him.

What a job Mum picked! she thought scornfully, changing into bathers and investigating the pool. It was a lovely pool, in a large, glassed-in room with windows facing a garden. There were floating toys and big plastic balls in the water. She cleared them to one side and enjoyed the luxury of having a whole indoor pool to herself. She swam about grandly, pretending she was Megan. Megan had a backyard pool, lucky thing. Megan's mother had never had to go out to work in her life. Megan had everything.

Half an hour later she became aware of a tapping on the centre window. Ben was out in the garden, peering worriedly in at her, his face against the glass. She ignored him, but he didn't go away, and the tapping became louder. She scowled, got out of the pool and opened the window.

"Listen, you!" she said. "I won't drown in this dumb pool! The water's hardly over my head, even down the deep end. Now nick off!"

"Ben drown one time," he said miserably.

"Oh, yeah? That's a bit hard to believe. Anyway, you're too chicken to even come in!" Shelley said crushingly. She jumped back into the water and did three laps, remembering proudly how it had felt when she won the medal last summer. She should have gone on with squad swimming; maybe she would have ended up swimming at an Olympic Games some day.

28

Ben was still at the window, watching. She tossed a red ball at him, hoping he'd take it and himself off. Ben didn't manage to catch the ball, but he fumbled about, picked it up and threw it clumsily back to her. Shelley threw it harder, and he missed again, but delightedly picked it up and returned it.

Shelley, bored, left the ball floating about in the water. Ben waited hopefully, his smile fading. "You bad girl, Kerry!" he said at last. "You not my girlfriend any more!"

"I never was!" Shelley said indignantly. "Get lost!"

But he stayed at the window.

"If you want that damn ball so much, you can come in and get it," she said. Ben stuck a leg in over the window sill, looked longingly at the ball bobbing about in the water, then pulled his leg back as though he thought the pool would surge up and engulf him. He made several despairing attempts to come in and fetch the ball, then hovered sadly outside the window, defeated.

Shelley sighed. He looked so glum standing there obviously expecting her to drown. There was a small plastic bucket floating about near the ball. She filled it with water and took it over to the window. "Water won't hurt you, you big dill," she said crossly.

Ben backed away, and his eyes didn't leave the bucket of water.

"You won't drown in a bucket," Shelley said, and

scooped up some water and splashed it over her head. She slicked the ends of her wet hair across her face like a mane, and made two donut holes and looked out at Ben. "Grrrr!" she said, teasing. "I'm a lion. GRRRRRRR!"

She wasn't prepared for his laughter, which was as large and spectacular as a circus procession.

"That's more like it," she said. "Water's nice."

Ben slowly crept his hand in through the window, cupped some water and trickled it warily on his head. It dribbled down inside his shirt collar. "Ben not

drown," he said, surprised, looking at the bucket of
pool water.

"No such luck," Shelley said.

The door opened and she turned quickly. A nurse
was coming in with three people behind her. Shelley
snatched up the clothes and towel she'd left by the side
of the pool and sped past them.

"You don't have to go, dear," the nurse called after
her. "You can stay here with us till your mother goes
off duty. It's quite all right."

But it wasn't all right, Shelley thought, hurrying
along the passage and out to the car. No way was she
going to share the pool with any of those scary
retarded people! If you could call them people!

CHAPTER FOUR

The bags of vegetables were heavy and Shelley was indignant with self-pity when she got home with them. Petra Van Rees never had to do any household shopping. She dumped the bags on the table and didn't offer to take the things out and put them away. The greengrocer had included a glossy calendar as a goodwill gift. It fell out and rolled across the kitchen floor. The pictures were all of improbably magnificent seascapes; the last one of a surfboard rider poised on the crest of a wave. Shelley prepared to put the calendar in with the waste paper collection.

"It's a waste to throw it out," Anne said. "Give it to Mrs Murray when she comes back from Albury." She was busy making paper streamers and Chinese lanterns, trying to do a million things at once. "They're to decorate the hostel tonight," she said. "We're having a disco party."

Shelley didn't want to hear about those freaks pretending to act like normal people. The whole idea of a disco was sick.

"Can I borrow some of your cassettes?" Anne asked, putting the finished streamers into a carton.

"My cassettes?" Shelley demanded, flaring. "I don't want their greasy fingerprints all over my cassettes, thanks very much!"

"Shelley, I wish you wouldn't be . . ."

"I had to save and save to get those cassettes! Why don't you pack up all my clothes, too, all of my things if it comes to that, and give the whole lot to those retards!"

"Shelley . . ."

"Why don't you just move in with them permanently, you're so rapt in spending all your time over there! You like them more than you like me, that's for sure! You don't even care about my holidays being all mucked up!"

She expected her mum to blaze right back at her, but Anne looked at her steadily for a long moment and said in a tired voice with no anger in it, "Shelley, why don't you grow up?"

Shelley went off and slammed the door of her room to disguise her shame. But the shame grew and grew to unbearable proportions. She still had the calendar in her hand. She picked up a Texta and printed "Ben" in vicious letters underneath the picture of the surfboard rider, as a sort of mean little joke. Then the shame rushed all through her, and scarcely aware of doing so, she made a few clumsy party hats out of the rest of the calendar pictures and went into the kitchen. She put the hats in with the streamers and balloons, not saying anything or looking at her mother.

When they got to the hostel, Anne was immediately surrounded in the foyer by people all babbling excitedly about the disco. Shelley slipped away down the corridor, before any of them could touch her or greet her in any way whatsoever. She got the key from the nurse's desk and felt someone breathing down her neck. She ignored him and opened the door to the pool.

"Jelly drown," Ben said mournfully. "I better come too."

"Listen, you!" she hissed through her teeth, then stopped because the nurse was looking at them both from her desk.

"It's okay, Shelley," said the nurse. "He'll just sit on the bench by the pool. When he gets tired of it, he can open the door from that side and come back out again, can't you, Ben? He won't go anywhere near the water. Goodness knows, we've all tried hard enough to coax him, but he just won't."

Shelley, fuming, barged ahead of him and got changed in the changing room. When she came out, Ben was sitting on the bench under the window. Edgy with anxiety, he watched everything she did in the pool. Shelley dropped hints about the disco, and what

he was missing out on, but he didn't go away. He just sat on the bench with his feet drawn up well away from any splashing, and watched over her. After a while he began to sing. Shelley found it excruciating. She couldn't make out the words, and his voice was strident and off-key. Every few minutes he stopped and told her she had to clap, and looked terribly hurt when she didn't.

"Your singing is just about on the same level as your swimming," she said nastily. Ben obviously didn't understand, thinking it was a compliment. Shelley put her fingers in her ears and thought wildly of ways to stop him singing. She suddenly remembered the surf calendar picture which she hadn't made up into a paper hat in case Anne noticed the writing on it. She'd stuffed that one guiltily into her beach bag. She scrambled out of the pool and thrust the glossy picture under Ben's nose. He stopped singing and looked at it.

"It's a picture of you," she said. "See, it's written underneath: B ... E ... N spells Ben."

Ben's eyes widened.

"And the rest of the writing underneath says you've got to go swimming in the pool," Shelley finished craftily, hoping it would scare him away, back to that travesty of a disco, where he belonged with those other shattered people. But he didn't go. He was suddenly too panic-stricken. He dropped the calendar picture as though it were red hot, backed into a corner of the bench and wrapped his arms about his head.

"Ben *drown*!" he whispered in anguish and began to cry.

Shelley stared at him, beginning to panic a little at being on her own. She wondered if she should ring the emergency bell on the wall and get a nurse to take him away, but she was scared of being scolded for upsetting him. He *had* to shut up! Anyone might hear the racket he was making and come to investigate, and she'd get into strife.

"It's okay," she said. "Hey, listen, don't cry! You don't have to be a surfie like that guy in the picture, not if you don't want to!" She tugged his hands away from his face and looked in consternation at the flowing tears. Clumsily she dabbed at them with a corner of her towel, feeling ridiculous, because he was twice her size. "No one could drown in that pool!" she said, tetchy with relief that he'd finally shut up. "I happen to be the boss of that pool, see, and I wouldn't let it drown anyone."

Ben looked so impressed that she started to show off. There was a wide step the width of the pool, leading down into the shallower end. Shelley walked backwards and forwards across the step, kicking the water about. "I'm the boss of the pool!" she crowed. "The water's a football! I'm Richmond playing against the pool, and I won! Look at the great goal I just kicked!"

She looked over her shoulder at Ben, and his face was bright with enchantment.

"Hey, come on," she said impulsively, and held out her hand.

The enchantment fled. "Ben drown!" he yelled, and his anger was like that of someone shaking the bars of a prison.

"Not if I hold your hand, you big sook!" Shelley stretched her hand further, and Ben slowly got up from the bench and took it. Shelley tugged him closer, until he was standing ankle deep in the water. "Come on, now," she ordered. "Walk up and down across the step, just like me. Come on, you can do it, and don't you dare say you'll drown!" He followed her jerkily, eyes clamped shut so he wouldn't have to look at the water. Shelley walked him slowly across the step, but when they reached the side, he snatched his hand away, darted back to the bench and pulled his feet up under him.

Shelley decided wrathfully to leave him there, ignore him and get on with her swimming, but then thought of his atrocious and persistent singing. She couldn't stand that again! She held out her hand and coaxed him back on to the step.

She walked him back and forwards across the width of the pool, over and over. She was stubbornly determined to make him do it on his own, without holding her hand.

It took an hour and a half.

At the end of that time, the bones in her hand felt cracked, but Ben was walking backwards and forwards across the step, ankle deep in water. All by himself.

"Ben *not* drown yet!" he said in awe.

"No, worse luck," Shelley said wearily, flexing her hand to get rid of the stiffness. "But if you want to look like that guy in the picture, you'll have to find yourself a pair of bathers."

CHAPTER FIVE

"My day off," Anne said. "I'm so tired I'm going to bed after lunch and staying there all afternoon."

"How will they manage at the hostel without you, even for one day?" Shelley asked sarcastically.

"They don't need any occupational therapy aides on Sundays," Anne said, too worn out to notice the sarcasm. "The parents always come and take the kids out."

Shelley moped about the house after lunch, glaring at the silent telephone which was useless for contacting any of her friends. They would all be away, or out, or occupied. She watched a tedious documentary on the television, then went round the block on her roller skates, seeing only doddering old Mr Harcourt tending his immaculate lawn. The whole quiet block seemed as restrictive as a prison. The rest of the summer holidays stretched barrenly before her. It was too hot to be racketing about the empty streets on roller skates; she could feel her socks growing clammy with sweat. It was a day for the beach, but even in her bored resentment, she hesitated to wake up Anne and demand to be taken there.

There was the council pool, but it was too far to walk, and the only connecting bus service didn't operate on Sundays. She flopped down in the back yard to take her skates off, but it wasn't an attractive place to linger. Her mother, working hard as the sole wage earner, had little time to spare for gardening.

Shelley thought suddenly of the blue-tiled pool at the hostel, tucked away by itself in its own private room. No one would be there; her mother had said that about parents coming on Sundays to take those kids out. And the nurses knew her by sight now. If she just strolled in, they'd smile at her in vague recognition. She could easily get the key and use the pool for as long as she liked, with no interruptions.

She collected her swimming things and went off by bike. When she reached the hostel, she chained the bicycle carefully to a side fence. She looked across at the glass door, and froze.

Ben was there, in his usual position, watching the cars go by. Maybe his parents were just late in coming to collect him, Shelley thought, but then she saw with irritation that he wasn't dressed for going out, anyhow. On the front of his tee shirt he wore the picture of the surfboard rider, stuck there with sticky-tape. His eyes painstakingly followed the course of each passing car. Almost, she thought, as though he expected each one to stop and the people get out and come in to visit him!

Gloomily she decided to go back home, but just as she was unfastening the bike, Ben spotted her. He made a joyful dive at the door, flung it open and grinned at her from ear to ear, with a smile like a slice

42

of watermelon. "Darry!" he cried over and over till her head rang.

"Shelley," she said. "I've already told you a million times! Can't you even say my name properly yet?"

She stepped around him and went along the corridor to the pool, knowing bitterly that he would follow her as closely as a shadow. "Listen," she said. "I want a proper swim in that pool today. I won't have time to baby-sit you and hold your hand while you walk up and down that rotten step. I'm going swimming and I mean it. That's all I came over here for, see? You'd better just stay out here where you can watch the nice cars."

He looked at her from under his fringe, like a cuffed dog. The sparkle went out of his eyes.

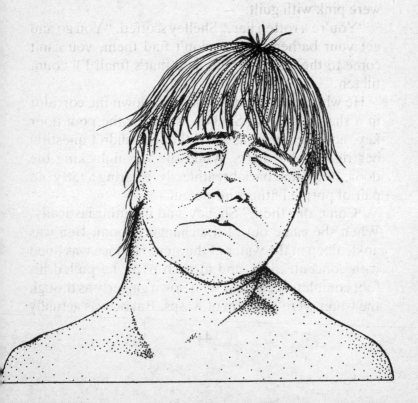

"You got your shorts and shirt all wet yesterday," she said tersely. "Those nurses will blame me if it happens again. Anyhow, what if your mum and dad show up to take you out? You'd better be waiting for them by the front door."

Ben shook his head slowly and sadly. No wonder his parents don't show up, she thought. If I had a kid who looked like him, I wouldn't show up, either! I'd just bung him in this place and forget about him!

"Okay," she said. "You can come to the pool with me. But you've got to go and find some bathers first."

Ben told her a rambling, uneasy story about how his bathers had been on the hostel clothes line and Tania had pinched them. But he told the story peeping out at her from laced hands, and the visible parts of his face were pink with guilt.

"You're a rotten liar," Shelley scoffed. "You go and get your bathers. If you don't find them, you can't come to the pool with me, and that's final! I'll count till ten."

He wheeled around and shot off down the corridor in a shambling run. Shelley asked for the pool door key, and the nurse, as she'd thought, didn't question her right to be there. While she was unlocking the door, Ben came back breathlessly, wearing a tatty old pair of purple bathers inside out.

"Come on, then," Shelley said unenthusiastically. When she came out of the changing room, Ben was ankle deep in the water at the step. His face was lined with concentration, and at each pace, he pulled his foot completely out and set it down gingerly as though the water were a swarm of wasps. But he was actually

44

walking backwards and forwards across the step all by himself.

Shelley jumped into the deeper end and showed off doing torpedoes. When she came up for air, Ben was looking at her wistfully. "It's about time you got off that stupid step and into the proper pool," she said.

"Ben drown!"

"Are you still on about that? You won't drown! I'm sick of telling you. You don't have to come right down here to this end where I am. Just get off the step and walk backwards and forwards across the pool up that end. The water's only up to your knees there, for crying out loud! Listen, if you do, I'll give you . . . I'll give you a silver star to bung on your surfie picture. How about that?"

A silver star! It was as if someone had lit two of them behind his eyes when she said it. Then he looked down at the water below the safe, wide step, and the stars flickered out.

"You won't drown! Look, I'll come up there and hold your hand like last time. I'm the boss of this pool and I don't let it drown people. All you have to do is get down from that step and walk, and the water will only come up to your knees. I won't let it come up any deeper than that. I'll be real proud of you if you do it, Ben!"

Proud of him? Shelley thought furiously. He's *nothing* to do with me! I don't care if he can't swim; if he has to stay on the sand when someone takes him to

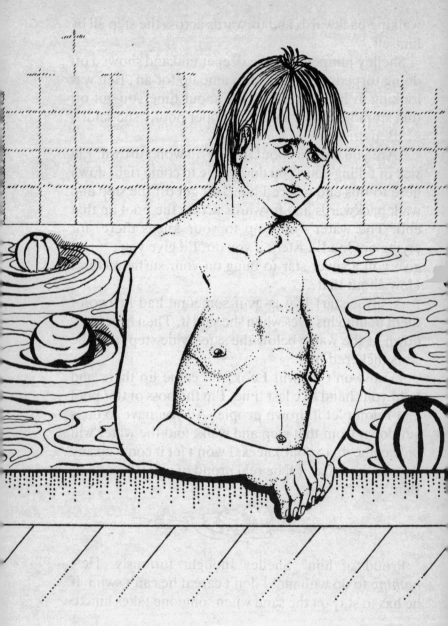

the beach . . . I don't even blame his mum and dad for not showing up today!

Ben, pale with effort, suddenly stepped down into the water.

"Wow, you did it!" Shelley cried. "I'm real proud of you! Now, all you have to do is walk back and forwards across the pool, right? Just the same as you did before on the step. No worries."

Ben kept his eyes shut and wretchedly shook his head.

"Go on! Think of that silver star I'll bring you tomorrow. You can be top dog around this place with a silver star. Aw, come on, Ben! Across the pool five times. Only five times, and I'll be holding your hand all the time, and then I'll let you get out."

She coaxed him across twice, then, when he was in the centre trembling in knee-deep water, she took her hand away and retreated to the deeper end and left him stranded.

"You can easily do it on your own," she said sternly. "You're a big guy, like in that picture. You show me how you can walk across all by yourself."

But while she was heckling him, she looked at his face. Never in her life had she seen a face so filled with terror. She stopped, and in the silence she found herself thinking with cold anger: Where the hell are his parents? Why didn't they show up and take him out? This whole place is empty and he's the only one left behind . . . How could they let him get to his age and be so scared of water along with everything else he's been loaded with! It's not . . . fair!

"Listen to me, Ben!" she said fiercely. "There's

nothing to be scared of. If you walk across five times, all by yourself, I'll write to the Richmond Footy Club and tell them about it. Honest! One time that whole team was here in this pool, and I gave them a silver star for walking across the pool and not hanging on to my hand. I'm the boss of this pool and I get to hand out silver stars to people. So I gave the Tigers one, but they had to pass the test first. Same as you. You'll pass it easy. Just think, you'll be walking around in the same water as the Richmond Tigers!"

Ben slowly put one foot in front of the other and traced a painful way to the side of the pool. He took one small step after another, one terrible step after another, and when he reached the side he stood there gasping.

Shelley brought her hands together above her head and clapped as though she had never seen anything so brilliant and dazzling. "Good on you, Ben!" she yelled, and her voice bounced off the tiled walls like fragments of reflected water and tumbled back into the pool. "On you, Ben! Even the Tigers didn't do it as good as that!"

Ben smiled at her through his fear and turned around and slowly walked back across the width of the pool. He did it five times, and at the end of the fifth time, he had stopped trembling.

Shelley looked at the clock above the door and scarcely believed that the whole exercise had taken nearly two hours. She got out of the pool and changed. She certainly didn't want her mother to find out where she'd been. If she found out, she might even think she *liked* coming over to this awful place!

48

Ben followed her, dripping, to the front door. He gazed out at her while she unchained her bike. Then he started to wave, to her, and to the people in the cars that passed by—the people who didn't wave back, and who never, never stopped.

Shelley rode down the street, discovering how difficult it was to steer a bike with one hand, and wave back to someone with the other.

CHAPTER SIX

Megan, suntanned and enviable with a whole lot of new summer clothes, chattered of nothing except what she'd done on her Gold Coast holiday. She didn't once ask Shelley what she had been doing, and Shelley suddenly found herself thinking that she didn't really like Megan, even though they were technically best friends and had gone all the way through school to Year Six together. Megan's rapid, egocentric voice hammered inside her head till it ached. She dutifully inspected all the new clothes; you always had to make a big fuss of Megan's new possessions. It was boring.

"I haven't shown you these terrific colour prints yet," Megan said. "There's some of me on water skis. Oh, and I've got to show you my new beach towel! It's fluorescent pink . . ."

"A fluorescent towel is silly," Shelley said. "What's the point of it? People don't go to the beach at night." It was really irritating, she thought, the way Megan was forever bragging and seeking attention.

50

"Let's go down to the mall and window shop," Megan said. "The sales are coming up soon. Let's pick out some jeans and stuff."

"No, I've just remembered I've got to go out somewhere important," Shelley lied. "Anyhow, you've got enough clothes already. Your wardrobe's stuffed with them."

"No one can have too many clothes!" Megan said indignantly. "And where are you going? You never go anywhere important."

But Shelley headed for home, drearily conscious that it was true; she never did go anywhere important. Maybe it would have earned her an invitation to stay the night at Megan's house, if she'd gone along to the shops and lavishly admired everything that Megan tried on. But she didn't think she could have stood a whole afternoon of that. Perhaps the hostel was preferable after all.

She remembered the promised silver star and turned back, groaning, to find a shop. She had to try three newsagencies before she found one that sold packets of silver stars.

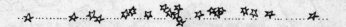

"All that lot are there waiting for you in the foyer," she said disagreeably when they reached the hostel that evening. "I don't know how you can stand the way they all crowd round and slobber all over you. That Tania makes me feel sick every time I look at her!"

"Tania can't help that birthmark," Anne said. "Anyhow, people don't have to be pretty to be nice looking."

"That doesn't make sense," Shelley said. "Course they do. Megan Webb's nice looking, and it's *because* she's pretty."

"I don't think Megan is pretty at all," said Anne, collecting things from the boot of the car. "Anyone as discontented and spoiled as Megan can't possibly be pretty. You have a good look at her sometime."

There was a folk guitar in the boot and several wooden recorders and a pair of castanets. "I borrowed them from various people," Anne explained. "We're having a music night. Tania loves guitar music, and I'm going to have a try at teaching her some chords."

Shelley stared through the glass door at Tania, with her pathetic ruin of a face. It seemed unbelievable that someone living behind a face like that could possibly know about guitars and music. Her mum was loopy, thinking that anyone who looked like that could learn music!

But it had nothing to do with her. Nothing at all. Any more than Ben had, hovering about wearing those awful old bathers with the frayed hems and loose threads hanging down. They looked ridiculous, and so did Ben, who followed her through the door to the pool, babbling on about silver stars.

"Nag, nag, nag," said Shelley. "Okay, I didn't forget, so you can stop earbashing. Where's your old surfie picture, then?"

Ben produced it, wrapped carefully in his towel, and Shelley told him to shut his eyes. Then she peeled one of the silver stars from the backing sheet and stuck it just above the head of the surfie in the picture. She hesitated and quickly peeled off two more, thinking that Ben really had earned them, walking across the pool yesterday. Walking through all that terror, all by himself.

"You can open your eyes now, Ben," she said.

He looked at the little row of silver stars and his delight was so immense that Shelley thought of Christmas presents piled beneath a tree, Easter eggs in the grass, brass bands, all occurring in the same time and place.

"Garn, they're only little paper stars!" she said, and jumped into the deeper end of the pool. "What are you waiting for, Mr Slowcoach? You going to stand there all night gawking at those little paper stars?"

Ben put the picture on the seat where it wouldn't be splashed, and trod carefully on to the step, and from the step down into the shallow end of the pool. He walked across five times and every time he reached the edge, he turned round and looked proudly at Shelley, making sure she had seen. His smile rekindled each time he made the crossing.

It's like he's swum the English Channel, Shelley thought, watching. As if he's sailed round the world all alone in a little teeny yacht.

"Hey, Ben!" she called out. "That's not such a big deal, walking across the pool down that shallow end. The water's only up to your knees. Listen. If you walk *along* the pool, down to where I am, I'll give you a *gold* star. What do you reckon about that? Only special people get gold stars."

Ben stood quiet and still.

"Richmond got one?" he asked at last.

"Nope. They never passed the test. Prince Charles and Princess Di tried, too, but they didn't make it, either, the big sooks. They chickened out half way, so I never gave them a gold star. I'm the only one who can hand out gold stars, because I'm the boss of the pool. I've got a medal at home to prove it."

Ben squinted down the length of the pool, and his face was raw with loneliness.

"Ben, there's nothing to it, walking along the side of the pool down to this end! Honest. All you have to do is walk along hanging on to the side, here to where I am and back to the step, five times. That's all you have to do to win the gold star."

Ben stared along the pool at her, as though she were on some distant planet.

"You won't drown," Shelley said. "I'm the boss of this pool, and it has to do everything I say. Ben, just think, a dirty big gold star! All those Tigers, the whole team, and not one of them was brave enough, not even the captain. I didn't give them a gold star. I've been saving it up for you, see!"

Ben slumped down on to the step in despair.

"Hey, look at you!" Shelley yelled. "You never told me you could sit down in the water like that! Strewth, you're a rotten big liar. You've only been kidding me that you're scared of water! Come on, get up off your backside and walk down to where I am!"

Ben shook his head numbly and put his hands over his face and rocked to and fro.

Shelley looked about for inspiration. She grabbed a

little plastic ship and skimmed it down to him across the pool's surface. Ben, startled, took his hands from his face and sent the ship back. Shelley returned it, taking care that it didn't quite reach him. Ben got off the step, reached forward and pushed the little ship towards her, completely captivated by the game. Shelley spun it cunningly back, making it stop just out of his reach.

Half way along the pool, where the water reached up to his waist, Ben grew aware of her trickery and stopped, panic stricken. He clung to the side and

howled with fright. He begged her to come and get him out of the pool.

"No I won't!" Shelley said. "And what's more, if you don't stop crying, I'll . . . I'll tell Tania what a baby you are! I'll tell all the nurses! I'll sit out the front of this hostel and stop all the cars going by and tell them, too. I'll bring them all down here to listen to that dumb stupid noise you're making! And I'll take away your surfie picture with the silver stars and give it to Tania!"

Ben took one quivering step and halted, clinging to the side like a frail old man.

"I'll write a letter to the Richmond Tigers and they won't let you barrack for them anymore! They'll come and take your teddy bear away and burn it."

Ben took one more haunted step.

"And if you don't walk down here, all the way down here, I . . . I won't ever come to see you anymore, and I won't be your girlfriend!"

Ben took a deep breath, shut his eyes and stumbled along the side of the pool, step by painful step. When he reached Shelley in the deep end where the water was up to his chest, he was as white as frost. Shelley reached up and put her arms around him and hugged him.

"There," she said gently. "Don't you cry, Ben. I told you you could do it! You're braver than Prince Charles and Princess Diana, and braver than all of Richmond footy team! I reckon you ought to be in a Grand Final all by yourself! I'm going to give you the whole packet of silver stars, because I'm real proud of you, Ben!"

She held him tight until he stopped trembling.

"Now," she said fiercely. "This is where I teach you
how to dog paddle."

CHAPTER SEVEN

Petra rang and yacked about her holiday at the horse ranch. "It was terrific!" she said. "What a pity your mum wouldn't let you come, too, Shelley."

"It wasn't a case of not letting," Shelley said belligerently. "It was because she couldn't afford it. I already told you that."

"What's the matter with you?" Petra demanded. "There's no need to snap my head off."

"Well then, you ought to listen a bit better when I tell you things. You and Megan, you're both the same. You never bother to listen to people."

"Do you want to hear about my horse riding holiday or not?" Petra said, offended. "It was really great. And next holidays, Mum said I can go to Norfolk Island with my Aunty Gwen."

She seemed to go somewhere spectacular every school holidays, Shelley thought. . . . Horse riding ranches, tours of Ayers Rock, once even to Bali. Every single holiday. That was because of that well-paid, time-consuming job her mother had managing the music shop in the city.

Petra didn't get to see much of her mother, Shelley thought suddenly. It was almost as though all those expensive holidays were like a string of apologies, perhaps even a bribe.

"So what have you been doing while I was away?" Petra said at last, in the middle of a breathless description of the holiday ranch marvels. But she didn't really sound interested in what Shelley had done.

"I went to a course in archery," Shelley lied. "It was beaut. I got a bullseye from fifty metres."

". . . there was this lovely pony there called Monty. Mum said . . ."

"And I went right out to sea on a fishing trawler," Shelley said.

". . . Mum said we might be able to buy Monty if I can find a paddock round here to keep him in."

There, she hadn't listened to one single word! "Come over to my house, Shelley, and watch TV. It's really boring being at home by myself. There's nothing to do here after being at that fantastic ranch. Did I tell you how I jumped Monty over . . ."

"I can't come because I'm busy," Shelley said. "I've got some shopping to do."

Anne was in the kitchen cutting out gingerbread men. "For tonight," she said. "The kids are going to decorate them. I would have liked to show them how to do the whole thing, mixing and baking and everything, but that cook over there is impossible. He makes such a fuss about anyone using the kitchen once he's tidied it up for the night. It's stupid that those kids can't use it. The craft room's locked up after 6.30 too,

60

for some reason. Very bad organisation. Oh, Shelley, I forgot to tell you, there's a full-time Recreation Officer's job becoming vacant soon, and I've applied for it. If I get it, I'll certainly make some changes over there! For a start, I'd try and do something about those ridiculous bed times. You know, they all have to go to bed at the same time, even the older ones like Catherine."

"Who's Catherine?" Shelley asked.

"The auburn-haired girl with glasses. She's nearly twenty and very sensible. I was playing cards with her last night, but one of those bossy nursing aides came and told her she had to go to bed. I tried to stick up for her, but I haven't got much say, seeing I'm just working there as a part-time casual. It's as though that place is run for the convenience of the staff instead of the residents. But it's going to be a different story if I manage to get that Recreation Officer's job!"

"Yeah, Mum," Shelley said. "You go sort them out. Listen, there's something I want to buy. Can I take some money out of my savings account?"

"You know I don't like you cutting into your savings account for rubbishy things, Shelley. Is it for clothes?"

Shelley nodded virtuously.

"Yes, all right then, I guess you can. You really haven't had much of a holiday this year, and I'm sorry about it. Buy yourself something nice. It can't have been much fun for you, having to trail over there with me every night and swim about in that old pool all by yourself for three hours. But it will be okay if I get that day job, you wait and see. Things will improve, including our finances."

"You're talking as though you've already got it," Shelley said.

"Well, I think I might have a chance. I heard on the grapevine that the committee has been really pleased with the work I've been doing in the evenings. One of the nurses told me that my name's on the short list for that job."

Shelley went over to the shopping centre and drew out twenty dollars of her meagre savings. She looked at the clothes on sale displays. She could certainly do with some new tops, or a new pair of sandals. There were lots of bathers on sale, too. Her bathers were getting tatty, almost as tatty, she thought, as those awful old purple ones of Ben's. His parents ought to buy him a new pair. But she remembered what Anne had told her: that Ben's parents hardly ever visited, rarely took him out or sent him new things.

She finished her shopping and went home.

Ben, she thought, deserved some sort of special award as well as a gold star, for not giving up in the pool yesterday. She shut the door of her room so that Anne couldn't come in and see what she was doing.

"What have you got in the parcel?" Anne asked curiously on the way to the hostel.

Shelley went pink and stuffed the parcel into her beach bag. "Nothing," she said. "And don't you start getting all bossy and nosey just because you think you've landed that posh job. Talk about a swollen head!"

"I'm allowed to have one," Anne said happily. "While you were out shopping, the hostel rang. I didn't really believe I'd have a chance against those

63

other applicants. I almost didn't apply, because some of them had fantastic references and qualifications. But . . . I've got the job and I start next week! I honestly don't know how I managed to swing it!"

I do, Shelley thought when they went into the hostel foyer. She stood back and watched her mother. Anne was surrounded by the residents, and Shelley saw clearly for the first time the joy in their faces at Anne's arrival. And it wasn't as though her mother was

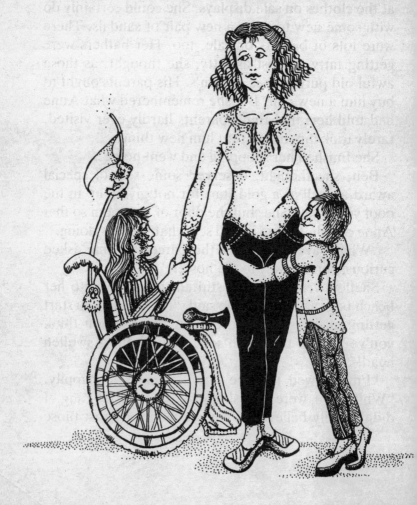

putting on an act for their benefit. She was her usual calm, quiet self, but you could easily tell what those people meant to her, and what she meant to them. Shelley thought shamefully of all the awful things she had said during those disjointed, patchwork holidays, and felt heavy with regret. She gave her mother an apologetic, impulsive hug. Anne looked surprised, "What's that all about?"

"Nothing in particular," Shelley said, embarrassed.

"Well, come back later when you finish in the pool, and we might give you one of our gingerbread men," Anne said. "Tania will ice a pair of bathers on one specially for you."

Shelley felt a stab of her old wariness, and thought uneasily that there was no way she could possibly eat a cake that Tania had touched.

She glanced swiftly at Tania, but instead found herself looking past the superficial disfigurement and into a pair of angelic blue eyes. Eyes that sparkled with friendliness. Maybe it was true, what her mother had said, that you didn't have to be pretty to be nice looking.

"Come on, Olympic Hope," she said to Ben, masking her confusion. "Think I've got all day, do you?"

In the pool room, she took the parcel from her beach bag and handed it to him, together with the gold star she'd found among the Christmas tree decorations at home. "Open the parcel in the changing

65

room," she ordered. "And be quick about it, else it might turn into a pumpkin."

She waited till he came out, and had to raise her voice to be heard above his excitement. "You've gone and put them on back to front," she said. "Typical. Here, give me those terrible old purple ones and I'll get rid of them."

Ben capered about in his beautiful new yellow and black bathers that had cost all of her twenty dollars, even at sale price. He'd stuck the gold star in his hair, and gazed at his reflection in the window panes, as proud as a Roman emperor. Shelley put the faded old bathers in a litter bin and clamped on the lid. She picked up Ben's surfboard rider picture and looked at it. He'd added the whole packet of silver stars, so that the surfboard rider looked as though he were riding the crest of a wave under a star-filled sky.

"You're nuts, Ben," Shelley said. "Quit showing off and for heaven's sake stop that awful singing! You've gawked at yourself in front of the window long enough. Time to get those new bathers wet. Race you to the end of the pool, one, two, three go!"

She only pretended to jump in, and drew back at the last moment, standing on the edge. But Ben jumped in with a splash that sent a noisy wave careering across the window panes. He didn't just wade to the end of the pool, but got down into the water and clumsily ploughed all the way to the deep end in his awkward attempt at dog paddling, copying her actions, the way she had shown him yesterday.

When he reached the end he turned round and saw her, still standing there, dry, on the step.

"You bad girl, Barry!" he yelled indignantly. "You cheat!"

"Shelley," she said. "How many times have I got to tell you? What are you going on about, anyhow? You won, didn't you?"

Ben stared at her, then stared down the length of the empty pool, and his face was filled with an immense, sudden joy.

"So come here and get your medal," Shelley said. She took it out of the beach bag where she'd hidden it so that Anne couldn't see it. Her swimming medal, won last summer at the club. Maybe the only one she'd ever win in her life, but that fact didn't seem important now. It had taken her all afternoon to scratch the words on the back, in her neatest lettering, using the point of a skewer.

"It says, '*Ben, Boss of the Pool*'," Shelley said, reaching up on tiptoe to put the cord of the medal round his neck. "No one else in the whole world has a medal like that. Not even Prince Charles or Princess Di. Not even the Tigers. And I'm going to be over every day after school, because my mum will be working here full-time starting next week. But I won't be dropping in just to see her. That's not the reason. It's because I'll have to make sure you're doing a proper job of being the boss of the pool! Like helping me teach Tania and Greg and Catherine and all that lot how to swim."

"I will!" Ben said, finally taking his eyes from the medal. "Just you watch me, Shelley!"

Then he ran around to the deep end and jumped in and did his clumsy, patient, beautiful dog paddle, up and down the pool five times.

All by himself, Shelley thought, watching. Swimming. Sort of. She couldn't see him very well because of the tears in her eyes.

ANOTHER OMNIBUS/PUFFIN BOOK

THE DEVIL'S STONE

Helen Frances

THE VALLEY had always lain in the shadow of the crag. Aboriginal legends spoke warily of the Old One who lived beneath it. There were tales of the mysterious disappearance of a child handed down from the earliest settlers and mention in an old diary of the *devil's stone* falling from the sky. When a huge rock suddenly appears in the valley, twins Emma and Leigh Tregarren find themselves caught up in a web of strange events which seems to be repeating a pattern from the past. As they struggle to understand what is happening in the valley, they are drawn into danger.

Set in the Adelaide Hills, *The Devil's Stone* is a fast-moving historical-fantasy with an intriguing and fascinating ending.

Commended, 1984 Australian Book of the Year. For children 11 years and up.

ANOTHER OMNIBUS/PUFFIN BOOK

EDGE OF FEAR

Helen Frances

When Lucy Talbot is pushed aside by a stranger in one of London's dark alleyways, she is not to know that this meeting will lead her on a desperate flight for freedom and survival half a world away in the wilds of Van Diemen's Land.

Silas Rudd is the ominous stranger, transported for murder years before and determined to settle an old score. Lucy is an orphan, equally determined to be reunited with her grandmother, who has settled in the islands of Bass Strait.

Together their quests take them on an uneasy journey through a world of treachery and violence, where secrets from the past are revealed and Lucy finds herself caught up in a web of revenge surrounding Rudd and an audacious convict woman, Nell Pillinger. In her struggle for survival, Lucy must search for new definitions of truth and justness in a society where savagery and natural justice prevail.

This exciting narrative from the authors of *The Devil's Stone* is recommended for children 11 years and up.

ANOTHER OMNIBUS/PUFFIN BOOK

THE SADDLER'S GRAND-DAUGHTER

Garry Hurle

In this trilogy of short stories Garry Hurle takes us back to a small rural community in the 1920s, when the days were as drowsy as sheep on a hot summer's afternoon, and life was as simple as it was spartan.

Francy is the saddler's ten year old grand-daughter, and from her we learn of the story behind the lost Super-duper Side Saddle; the magical properties of the Cheeky Stockwhip; and the hidden beauty of the Gum Nut Reins — all lovingly made by her grandfather, the saddler.

This is a gentle book, full of fun and adventure, delight and humour.